Nature CAT ™

BACKYARD EXPLORER'S

T0079223

BuzzPOP

Disclaimer: Nature Cat and his pals are cartoon animals. Check with an adult before bringing along a pet on your next outdoor adventure.

BuzzPop

an imprint of Little Bee Books

New York, NY
Written by Jesse McMahon
Copyright © 2021 by Spiffy Entertainment, LLC.
Nature Cat® and associated characters, trademarks and design elements
are owned by Spiffy Entertainment, LLC., 2017 Spiffy Entertainment, LLC.
All rights reserved, including the right of reproduction in whole or in part in any form.
BuzzPop and associated colophon are trademarks of Little Bee Books.
Manufactured in China TPL 1220 | First Edition

1 3 5 7 9 10 8 6 4 2

ISBN 978-1-4998-1141-4

buzzpopbooks.com

For information about special discounts on bulk purchases, please
contact Little Bee Books at sales@littlebeebooks.com.

CONTENTS

Where to begin?

MEET YOUR GUIDES

Onward and yonward!

NATURE CAT

When his owners leave for the day, this house cat becomes a backyard explorer!

Viva la nature!

SQUEEKS

Always up for adventure, this mouse knows every animal in town.

Hi! It's me, Hal!

Oh yeah! Oh yeah!

DAISY

The brainiest of the bunch, this bunny loves gardens and facts.

HAL

Meet the most loyal, lovable, and huggable dog ever!

WELCOME, NATURE LOVER!

'Tis I, Nature Cat! Together with my friends, we will explore the great outdoors. Why, look! It is right outside your door.

There are plants growing wild. There are animals being amazing. There are rocks ready to show us how they were made!

All we need is our eyes, ears, noses, and tails. We will find out what nature needs. We will help nature. And, we will ask great, big questions.

Are you ready to become a Backyard Explorer?

Tally ho!

Oooh! A bird! I wonder why it's singing.

BACKYARD EXPLORER'S CHECKLIST

Before you head outdoors, make sure you:

- [ ] Check with an adult.
- [ ] Dress for the weather.
- [ ] Put on sunscreen and bug spray.
- [ ] Gather the right tools and supplies for your nature adventure.
- [ ] Pack a snack and fill your water bottle. Choose reusable containers!
- [ ] Grab your Backyard Explorer's Guide and a pencil.
- [ ] Say the Backyard Explorer's promise on your poster.

DISCOVER PLANTS!

Let's take a look at plants. Sweet!

Plants are living things. They make their own food using sunlight. Some plants are smaller than a grain of rice. Some plants are taller than the Statue of Liberty.

Oh baby, I wonder which plant smells the sweetest!

HIP HIP HOORAY FOR TREES!

Trees are the biggest plants on Earth. Some trees live for hundreds or thousands of years. Trees offer shade, shelter, a place to climb, and space for a nest.

Deciduous (dih-SID-juh-wus) trees have leaves. In the autumn, the leaves change color and fall off the tree.

deciduous

leaf

branches

crown

trunk

root

I'd like to see a whole forest of these trees!

Evergreen (EH-vr-green) trees have needles. The needles stay green all year long.

evergreen

crown

branch

needles

trunk

root

THE KINGDOM OF THE ROTTING LOG

What happens after a tree dies? It becomes food for bugs and other little critters. The critters help to turn the different tree parts into soil. Soil is where a new tree can grow!

Check this out! Rotting logs are like nature's recycling center.

Draw trees you've seen!

LOOK CLOSER:

Does the tree have pointy needles for leaves? If it does, it's an evergreen. If it has flat leaves, it is deciduous!

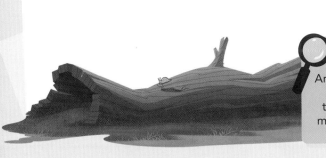

LOOK CLOSER:
Are there holes in the tree?
Is there a nest in
the branches? An animal
might be living in the tree!

WHAT'S IN A LEAF?

Just like you, plants need food for energy to live and grow. Most plants make their own food using a process called **photosynthesis** (foh-toh-SIN-thuh-sis). The three main ingredients are:

1. energy from the Sun's light

2. an invisible gas from the air

3. water

The action happens in the plant's leaves!

??? DID YOU KNOW:
The food that leaves make is sugar! Sweet!

IT'S NOT EASY BEING GREEN

When the leaves on trees turn bright yellow, orange, or red, that usually means it's autumn. Soon, the leaves will fall to the ground. Then, winter will come. When spring rolls around, the trees will grow new, green leaves.

Who knew leaves were so fancy?

Have you seen any of these leaves? Check them off!

oak ☐
Look for a leaf with wavy or spiky edges.

rosebush ☐
Look for an oval shape.

maple ☐
It has five points!

pine ☐
Surprise! The needles on evergreen trees are a kind of leaf.

dandelion ☐
They are long, thin, and rough.

13

Draw leaves you've seen!

🔍 **LOOK CLOSER:**

Did you find a leaf on the ground? See if you can match it to the leaves on a nearby plant.

🔍 **LOOK CLOSER:**

Can you see lines in the leaves? Those are called **veins** (vay-ns). They bring water from the plant into the leaves. They also bring sugar from the leaves to the rest of the plant!

SEEDS, GLORIOUS SEEDS!

Seeds come from flowers, fruits, and cones. Some seeds are as tiny as the period at the end of this sentence. Some seeds are bigger than your head! After seeds form, they travel away from the plant. What grows out of a seed? A plant!

How does a seed travel with no legs?

TRAVELING SEEDS

Dandelion seeds float through the air. Pine cones can roll on the ground or float on the water. They carry pine tree seeds! Seeds in fruit can get eaten by wild animals. The seeds end up in a new place when the animal poops them out! Some seeds can stick to animals. Then the seeds fall off in a new place.

Have you seen any of these seeds? Check them off!

☐ **maple**

This seed's pod is called a helicopter.

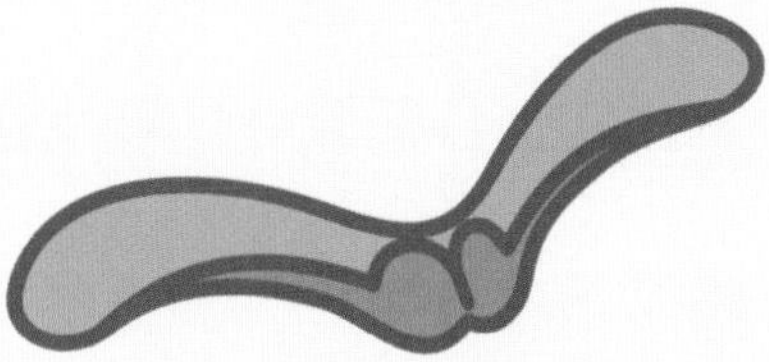

☐ **dandelion**

Look for the fluffy puffs. Each piece of fluff has a seed!

☐ **bean**

Peek inside a bean pod or peapod. Those are seeds!

☐ **oak**

This seed is called an acorn.

☐ **apple**

The seeds are in the core of the apple.

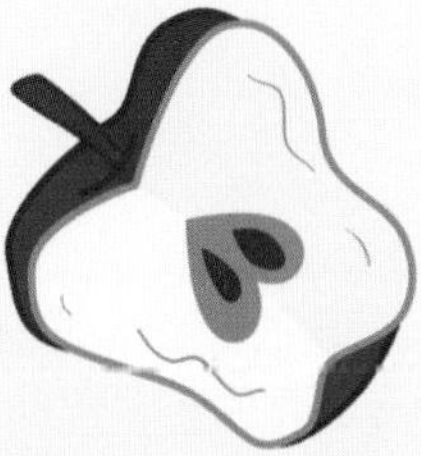

☐ **pine**

Pine cones have pine tree seeds inside!

Draw seeds you've seen! What plant do you think the seed will grow into? Draw the plant, too!

TRY IT:

Drop a pine cone in water. The pine cone will close its scales. Then the seeds are safe!

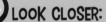**LOOK CLOSER:**

Does the seed have spikes on the outside? It might travel by sticking to an animal.

Tah-dee! Hello there, little seeds, it's me, Hal!

TRY IT:

Ask an adult to cut into a fruit. Can you find the seeds?

LET'S SPROUT A SEED!

You can see a bean seed sprout, or grow. In about 10 days, you will see roots growing down and a stem growing up! Congratulations, you have helped a new plant grow!

Materials: Bean seed, a paper towel, water, and a small, clear container

Steps:

1. Fold the paper towel and wrap it around the inside of the container.

2. Dampen the paper towel.

3. Place the seed between the paper towel and the container's side about halfway up from the bottom.

4. Put the container in a warm, sunny spot. Keep the paper towel damp.

5. Wait for it to sprout!

WILDFLOWER ROUNDUP

Wildflowers are flowers that were not planted by people. They grow in meadows. They grow along the road. They even grow in sidewalk cracks! Wildflowers are food for birds, bees, and other animals.

Let's round up some wildflowers. Yee-haw!

ALERT!

Do you want to help wildflowers? Draw wildflowers. Don't pick them. The flower is how the plant makes seeds. Leave the flower where it is. When it is ready, it will drop seeds. Then, more wildflowers can grow.

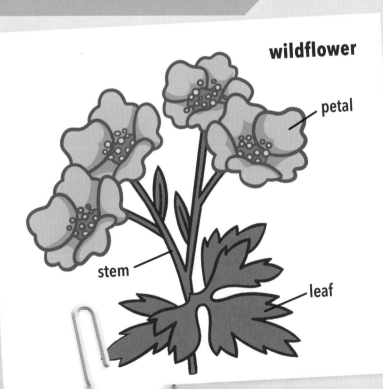

wildflower

petal

stem

leaf

Have you seen any of these wildflowers? Check them off!

buttercup ☐

Count five rounded petals. They are yellow like butter!

violet ☐

Look for leaves in the shape of a heart. The petals are purple or blue.

Queen Anne's lace ☐

Too many flowers to count on one stem?
Are they white with a black spot?
You found it!

Draw wildflowers you've seen!

LOOK CLOSER:

Do you see yellow dust in the flower? That's pollen. That helps the plant make seeds!

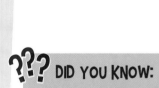

??? DID YOU KNOW:

Some caterpillars can only eat the leaves of one kind of plant! Monarchs only eat milkweed leaves.

LOOK CLOSER:

Is the plant standing tall? Even in the wind? Roots are holding the plant in place. The roots help keep the soil in place, too.

USE YOUR NOSE:

Does the flower smell sweet? The nice smell attracts bees. Bees spread pollen from one flower to another.

Ready, set, draw!

LOOK CLOSER:

Do you see creatures nearby? Butterflies, bees, and some kinds of birds drink the nectar inside flowers. Caterpillars eat the leaves.

LET'S COMPOST

Compost is broken-down plant and animal matter. You can add compost to the soil in your garden. This helps your plants grow!

You can make a simple composter to see how it works. Here's what you'll need:

- Empty, clean, see-through plastic two-liter bottle
- Shredded newspaper and dead leaves
- Small handful of dirt from outside
- Kitchen and yard scraps, such as grass clippings, vegetable scraps, eggshells, or coffee grounds
- Small tray to hold your composter
- Spray bottle with water

Let's compost!

1. Have an adult cut off the top of the bottle, and punch small holes along the sides and bottom of the bottle. Save the top.

2. Place the bottle on the tray.

3. Add your first layer of dirt, shredded newspaper, and old leaves.

4. Spray with water.

5. Add kitchen scraps and other compost materials. Do not add dairy or meat.

6. Put the top back on, but upside down, so it is a funnel through which you can add scraps or some water if it looks dry.

7. Place your composter in a sunny place. Keep adding scraps, give it a stir every few days, and let it rot!

8. When it looks like dirt, you can add it to your garden!

When it's done, it'll smell like . . . wait for it . . . soil!

LET'S SAVE THE VEGGIES

Fruits and vegetables are parts of plants. Plants grow in different ways. Sometimes carrots can be twisted. Potatoes can be dimpled. Apples can be lumpy. The secret: They still taste just as delicious. Celebrate nature by picking the ugly fruit or vegetable.

> I don't see what's so bad about these funny-looking vegetables. I call this one Bumpy. Hi, Bumpy, I'm Hal!

NO LAUGHING MATTER!

Funny-looking foods often end up in the trash. What a waste!

DISCOVER ANIMALS!

Animals are living things. They eat food and drink water. Birds, insects, reptiles, fish, amphibians, and mammals are animals. They all play important roles on the planet.

Dolphins are mammals, like you.

Mammals with fins? What's next? Mammals with wings?

ANIMAL SIGNS

When you walk through mud, snow, or wet sand, you leave behind footprints. It's a sign you were there. Animals leave signs, too. Sometimes they leave tracks with their feet. Sometimes they leave behind tufts of fur, feathers, the hulls of seeds, or maybe even a nest or eggs! What will you find?

OPEN YOUR EYES, EARS, AND NOSE

When you are looking for animal signs, look all around you. Is that a tuft of hair caught on a piece of bark? Listen quietly. Was that the rat-a-tat-tat of a woodpecker pecking? Smell with a deep breath in. Is that Hal refusing to take a bath again?

ANIMAL SIGNS AT NIGHT

Some kinds of animals are **nocturnal** (nock-TERN-uhl). That means they are busy at night. They have special features. Some have large eyes. Some have a good sense of smell. Some have strong hearing. These features help them get around in the dark.

Have you heard or smelled any of these animals? Check them off!

Tune in with your ears to hear and your nose to smell an animal at night.

owl ☐

hoot

gray treefrog ☐

trill

bat ☐

squeak

raccoon ☐

ee-ee-ee

skunk ☐

BEES, BUTTERFLIES, AND OTHER POLLINATORS

A **pollinator** (PAHL-n-ay-tr) is an animal that moves pollen from one plant to another. Pollen is the yellow, sticky powder on a plant. It helps a plant form seeds.

bee	moth	hummingbird	butterfly

 **DID YOU KNOW:**
Pollen may make you sneeze.

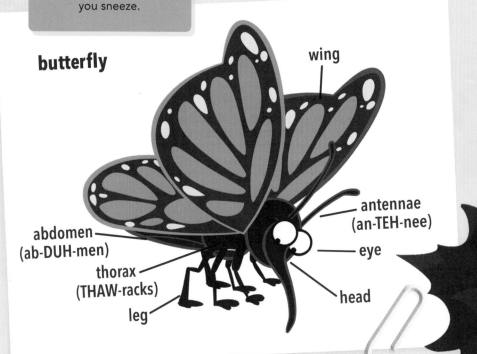

butterfly

wing

antennae (an-TEH-nee)

eye

head

abdomen (ab-DUH-men)

thorax (THAW-racks)

leg

Pollinators help plants make fruits and vegetables. That's the food we eat! These critters are small, but they have a big job. That's why Squeeks is all abuzz for pollinators!

You may hear a bee before you see it.

Can you hear the buzz, man?

CATERPILLARS!

A caterpillar is a young butterfly or moth. Look on plants for caterpillars. You may also see a **cocoon** (kah-KOON) on a plant. Inside a cocoon may be a caterpillar. A cocoon protects the caterpillar as it changes into a moth. When it leaves the cocoon, it is an adult. Check out those wings!

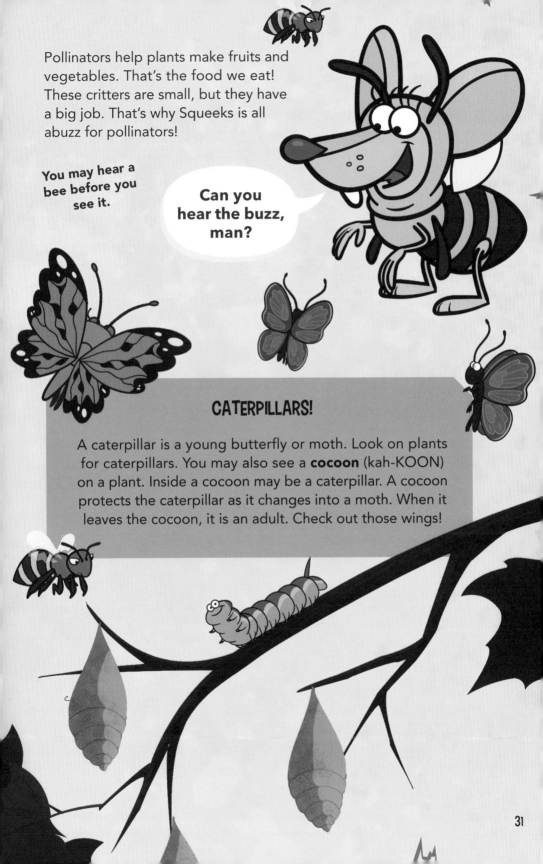

Draw bees, butterflies, and other pollinators you've seen!

LOOK CLOSER:

Does the pollinator
have six legs?
It's an insect.

LOOK CLOSER:

Does the pollinator
have feathers?
It's a bird!

LOOK CLOSER:

Does the pollinator only eat from one kind of plant? Make sure to keep that plant around!

LOOK CLOSER:

How does it eat? A butterfly or moth has a long **proboscis** (pro-BAA-suss). It is like the snout of an elephant. Birds that drink nectar have long beaks. A proboscis or long beak helps the critter eat the nectar in a flower.

33

FIREFLIES A-GLOW

Fireflies are beetles. Beetles are insects. Some fireflies make light using a special organ! They flash the light in a pattern. That is how they share information with other fireflies

KNOW THE GLOW!

Most kinds of animals that make light live in very dark places. They live deep in the ocean and in caves. Some animals use light to attract animals to eat. Some use light to scare away other animals.

We found this cool guy on a warm summer night, baby! But after we said "hello," we made sure to let it *a-go*.

When you are looking for an insect, count the legs! Insects have six legs.

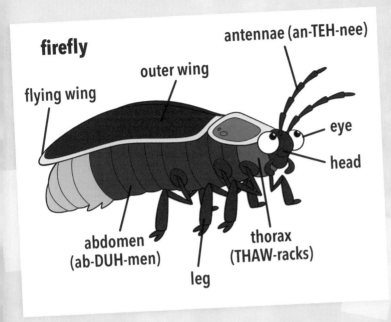

firefly

flying wing

outer wing

antennae (an-TEH-nee)

eye

head

abdomen (ab-DUH-men)

thorax (THAW-racks)

leg

The firefly's outer wings are hard. They protect the set of wings used for flying.

Fireflies aren't the only insects around! Check off the insects you've seen!

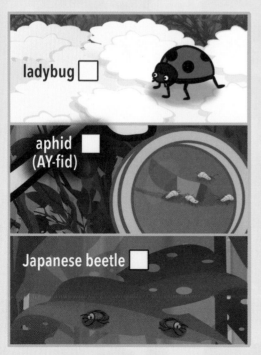

ladybug ☐

aphid ☐
(AY-fid)

Japanese beetle ☐

Holes in leaves are signs of aphids and Japanese beetles. They eat leaves for lunch! And breakfast and dinner.

Draw fireflies, ladybugs, and other insects you've seen!

LOOK CLOSER:
Check out those antennae! They help an insect sense the world around them.

LOOK CLOSER:
Can the insect walk straight up walls? Some insects have hairs, claws, or sticky liquid on their feet to help them climb.

LOOK CLOSER:

Is the insect alone? Some insects work as part of a group. Ants do this. A group of ants is called a **colony** (call-EH-nee). Different ants have different jobs in the group. The same is true for some kinds of bees!

USE YOUR EARS:

Is the insect making a sound? Many kinds of insects share information by scent, movement, or light. Some insects share information by making sounds. Male crickets chirp to attract female crickets.

A MIGHTY HUNTER

What has eight legs and can be a big help in the garden? The yellow garden spider! The yellow garden spider spins a large web. It uses the web to catch bugs. Some of these bugs are pests that eat Daisy's plants.

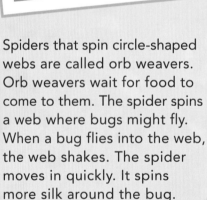

Spiders that spin circle-shaped webs are called orb weavers. Orb weavers wait for food to come to them. The spider spins a web where bugs might fly. When a bug flies into the web, the web shakes. The spider moves in quickly. It spins more silk around the bug. Then it's mealtime!

??? DID YOU KNOW:

Spiders are part of a group of animals called **arachnids** (uh-RACK-nidz). Do you see a bug with eight legs? You have found an arachnid.

Sometimes a spider needs to build a new web. To do that, it starts by eating what is left of the old web. The spider's body uses the old silk to make a new web. It's recycling in action!

Can you draw a yellow garden spider?

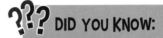 **DID YOU KNOW:**
All spiders make silk. But not all spiders spin webs.

Granny Bunny here! Most spiders aren't dangerous, but you should look at a spider rather than touch it.

ZE WORM WHISPERER

Many kinds of tiny critters live under the soil. One kind is earthworms! Earthworms help keep the soil healthy. They turn it over like little plows. They also eat dead things, such as plants. An earthworm's poop gives the soil **nutrients** (NEW-tree-ints). Nutrients help new plants grow.

SLUGS AND SNAILS

Slugs and snails break down dead things, too. Look for slugs and snails in damp places. Try looking under rocks or in the grass or garden after it rains.

Have you seen any of these critters? Check them off!

earthworm ☐

You might have
to dig to see an
earthworm.

snail ☐

Spy snails on the
ground after it
rains.

slug ☐

Look for slugs
under rocks.

Draw what you discovered below.

Bonjour, I
am Ze Worm Whisperer.
Our wormy friends need to be
covered by ze damp soil. It hides
zem from ze Sun. It also keeps
zem from becoming
bird food!

READY FOR REPTILES?

Snakes, turtles, and lizards are all examples of reptiles. Reptiles have no fur or feathers. Reptiles are all cold-blooded. This means they can't make their own body heat. They bask in the sun to warm up, or find a shady spot when they need to cool down.

IS THAT MY EGG?

Most reptiles lay eggs. The eggs are usually round. They may have a soft, leathery shell or a hard shell like a bird's egg. A turtle may bury her eggs in the soft dirt. A snake may lay her eggs in or under a rotting log. A lizard may drop her eggs in a hole in a garden.

Reptiles shed their skin. Be on the lookout for snake skins around rocks, logs, and other places snakes like to hide.

Have you seen any of these reptiles? Check them off!

lizard ☐
A dry, sunny rock is a good place to find lizards.

snake ☐
Watch where you step! Sometimes snakes are on the ground.

turtle ☐
A pond is a great place to find turtles.

Draw reptiles you've seen!

LOOK CLOSER:
Does the reptile have claws? What might the claws help it do?

LOOK CLOSER:
Is the reptile sitting still in the sun? It might be basking to warm up!

LOOK CLOSER:

Reptiles have thick skin or scales. Some also have a shell on part of their bodies.

LOOK CLOSER:

Is the reptile the same color as anything around? Blending in helps animals hide. That's called **camouflage** (KAM-uh-flaazh).

INTRODUCING THE AMAZING TOAD!

Toads are amphibians (am-FIB-ee-inz). They are also cold-blooded. This means they can't make their own body heat. Toads can do many things! Some toads can sing for 20 seconds. Some toads can lay 20,000 eggs. But no toad can give you warts!

THERE'S A FROG IN MY TOAD

Did you know toads are a kind of frog? Here are some tips to help you know whether you are looking at a toad.

- Toads have short legs.
- Do you see webbed feet? If not, it's likely a toad.
- Toads hop or walk.
- A toad's skin looks bumpy.
- Toads spend most of their lives on land.

Can you draw a frog and a toad?

Well, that's more eggs than I can count, Madam Toad!

ONE TOUGH BIRD!

Many birds fly south in the fall. But some birds stay put! Meet the chickadee. When the weather gets cold, these birds trap heat with their feathers. They store food and roost in small spaces away from the cold and wind. Chickadees visit backyard bird feeders often. They need to eat a lot to make it through the cold winter nights.

CHICKADEE-DEE-DEE-DEE

Birds can be hard to spot. But you can hear birds easily! Birds sing and make sounds to communicate. Birds make sounds to attract mates. The chickadee makes a chick-a-dee-dee-dee sound to say, danger!

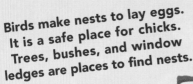

Birds make nests to lay eggs. It is a safe place for chicks. Trees, bushes, and window ledges are places to find nests.

Have you seen any of these birds? Check them off!

Draw birds you've seen!

LOOK CLOSER:

Is the bird pecking the ground? It may be looking for bugs and worms to eat!

LOOK CLOSER:

Does the bird have a twig in its beak? It may be building a nest.

LOOK CLOSER:
Are many birds
flying in one group?
That's a flock.

Weird!
I use my tongue
to take a bath.

LOOK CLOSER:
Is the bird splashing in water
or rolling around in dust?
It may be taking a bath!

51

FURRY FRIENDS

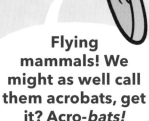

Mammals (MAM-uhlz) are animals that have fur and feed on their mother's milk. You are a mammal! Bats are the only mammals that can fly. Some kinds of bats eat insects. Some kinds of bats eat the nectar of flowers. These bats are pollinators! They help pollinate bananas, peaches, and mangoes. Thanks, bats!

Flying mammals! We might as well call them acrobats, get it? Acro-*bats!*

CALLING ALL BACKYARD EXPLORERS!

Bats are in trouble and need our help. Their habitats are disappearing. Bat boxes are one way to help bats. This gives them a safe, dark, warm place to hibernate, sleep, and raise their young.

bat box

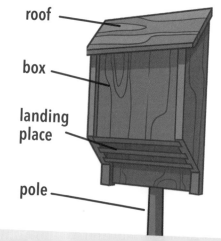

roof

box

landing place

pole

Have you seen any of these mammals? Check them off!

beaver ☐
Spot a beaver by a pond.

mouse ☐
Listen for squeaks in the night.

porcupine ☐
Find him in the forest.

squirrel ☐
Hear them chattering in parks!

deer ☐
They like wooded areas.

Beavers have teeth that don't stop growing. They gnaw on wood to keep their teeth from getting too long.

Male deer shed their antlers each year. Then they grow new ones!

Draw mammals you've seen!

LOOK CLOSER:

Does the animal have a long tail? It might help the animal balance.

LOOK CLOSER:

Long legs and hooves help animals move fast and travel far.

54

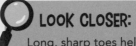

LOOK CLOSER:

Long, sharp toes help
animals grip or climb.

LOOK CLOSER:

You might spot a porcupine quill
on the ground. But, porcupines
can't shoot their quills!

THE DARING DRAGONFLY

The dragonfly can fly up, down, sideways, and backwards. It can even stay in one place in the air, like a helicopter. The dragonfly lives near water. It catches bugs with its feet. Then it eats them!

??? DID YOU KNOW:

The dragonfly can see very well. Its big eyes can see in almost every direction. A dragonfly can't see what's right behind it, though!

head

eyes

dragonfly

thorax

wings

legs

abdomen

A dragonfly starts out as an egg in water. When it hatches, it is a **nymph** (nimf). The nymph has no wings. It swims very fast, eating other young bugs. It also may eat tadpoles and small fish. As it grows, the nymph sheds its skin many times. This is called "molting." In its final molt, the dragonfly nymph becomes an adult dragonfly.

nymph

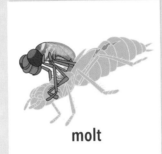

molt

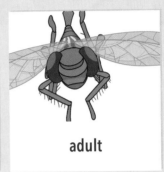

adult

When you see something that looks like a bug with no insides, it might be the skin of a dragonfly nymph.

Can you draw an adult dragonfly or a nymph?

LET'S LOOK UNDER THE WATER

A pond viewer will help you see critters under the water!

Onward and pond-ward!

You'll need:

- an empty cardboard milk container
- safety scissors
- waterproof tape or a strong rubber band
- clear plastic wrap

SOMETHING'S FISHY

Fish live in the water. They breathe using gills. Fins help them move through the water. Some fish, such as trout, eat dragonfly nymphs!

Follow these steps:

1. Ask an adult for help to cut the top and bottom off the milk carton.

2. Cut enough plastic wrap to cover the bottom of the carton.

3. Pull the wrap tight and attach it with tape or the rubber band.

4. The plastic wrap side will go in the water.

Is it just the twinkling in my eyes or are there more stars tonight?

DISCOVER ROCKS, WATER, AND MORE!

Rocks, soil, and water are nonliving things. They are important parts of the environment. They affect how plants and animals live and grow!

WATER REALLY IS AMAZING

Water!

Why does it always have to be water?

Sorry, Nature Cat! Water is a big deal! Check out all the things it can do. Water that flows through rock can make a canyon or a cave. When water becomes ice, it can make rocks crack and the ground swell. And don't forget, all living things need water to survive!

WATER IN ALL ITS FORMS

Liquid: Think of **water** in a cup, puddle, or stream. It splashes and flows. It can't hold a shape. A liquid goes to the edge of whatever holds it.

Gas: There is water you can't see all around you. It floats in the air. It's called water **vapor**. It makes air feel damp.

Solid: When water cools to 32° Fahrenheit, it becomes solid, **ice**! A solid can hold its own shape. An ice cube is a cube no matter where it is!

Have you seen water in any of these forms? Check them off!

A **cloud** forms when tiny water droplets and ice crystals come together in the sky. ☐

Fog is a cloud that is near the ground. You may see fog when the ground is warmer than the air. ☐

Hail is balls of ice that fall from the sky. You may see and hear hail fall during a thunderstorm. ☐

Rain falls when the water droplets in a cloud grow and become too heavy. ☐

A **puddle** forms after rain falls. They dry up in the sun! ☐

A **stream** or **river** is a body of water. The water in it flows! ☐

Draw water you've found in nature! Have you splashed in a puddle? Have you caught a falling snowflake? Have you watched clouds in the sky?

KEEP WATCH:

Is the water there every day? And does the water flow? It may be a stream or a river!

KEEP WATCH:

Does the water come and go? It may be a kind of weather!

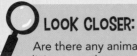

LOOK CLOSER:
Are there any animals
living near the water?
Water is important
to share!

LOOK CLOSER:
Is the water you found
a solid or liquid?
Hint: Clouds are a mix!

ROCK STARS

Rocks are some of the oldest things on Earth. They can be huge like boulders. Water and wind can break rock into tiny pieces. Those pieces become sand or part of the dirt beneath your feet. Rocks look and feel different because they are made of different material. They are also made in different ways.

??? DID YOU KNOW:

Every rock has a story. See the lines on this rock? Those are the rock's layers that were pressed together over a really, really long time!

This rock was formed by pressure, man.

STUCK ON YOU

Lodestone is a type of rock. Thousands of years ago, people discovered that lodestone attracts iron. That makes it a magnet! Magnets played a part in many important inventions, including the compass! A piece of lodestone hanging from a string will point towards north.

Have you seen any of these rocks? Check them off!

Quartz is bumpy or lumpy. It can be clear, white, or other colors.

A **geode** is a rock with crystals inside.

A **river** rock is made smooth by water. This one is a perfect skipping stone!

A **meteorite** is a space rock. A museum is a good place to see one.

Obsidian (uhb-SI-dee-uhn) is a rock formed by the lava of a volcano.

Draw rocks you've seen!

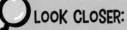

LOOK CLOSER:

Is the rock sparkly?
Different minerals
in rocks make
them shine.

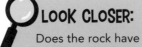

LOOK CLOSER:

Does the rock have
pointy, round, or
flat edges?

USE YOUR HANDS:

Is the rock very hard?
Or can you break it
apart with your fingers?

LOOK CLOSER:

Is the rock one color?
Or does it have
many colors?

MAGNIFICENT MUD

A little soil plus a little water makes mud! Mud helps beavers build dams. It helps birds build their nests. Pigs, elephants, and other animals take baths in mud. It helps them stay cool, free from bugs, and protected from the Sun.

Mud is mud-nificent! Is that a word?

FUN WITH MUD!

Nature Cat and his friends paint with thin mud. They make sculptures with thick mud. They walk through the mud to make squish, squish, squish sounds. They even slide through the mud and make mud angels.

Have you seen any of these types of mud? Check them off!

Sandy mud pours through your fingers easily when you squeeze it. It's perfect for making dribble castles.

Silty mud is colorful and slippery. You can use it as paint!

Clay mud is sticky, heavy, and stays together. Try shaping it into a bowl.

??? DID YOU KNOW:
People have used mud for building houses, making cups, and much more.

Draw your mud-nificent adventures!

TRY IT:

Make a sandcastle with really wet sand. Make another with moist sand. Make another with dry sand. Which one holds together better?

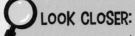

LOOK CLOSER:

Have you seen mud of different colors? Mud's color comes from the minerals in the soil.

TRY IT:

Make a footprint in the mud. Was it easy or hard to pull your foot out of the mud?

USE YOUR HANDS:

Do you think your mud has more clay, silt, or sand?

SUN AND SHADOW

A shadow happens when an object blocks the light. You can see shadows outside on sunny days. Watch how shadows grow longer or shorter throughout the day.

TRY IT:

When you want to make a shadow, stand with the Sun or other light behind you. You'll see your shadow in front of you.

Hi, Hal's shadow! It's me, Hal.

When you sit in the shade, you are sitting in a shadow. Trees, cliffs, mountains, and sand dunes all cast shadows to make shade in the natural world. The shade protects you from the Sun. It is a place to cool down on a hot day. A shady, damp place is where you may see moss or mushrooms. You might even see a snake cooling down after basking in the Sun.

Draw what you've discovered in the shade!

TALLY HO, A RAINBOW!

When a rainstorm rolls away, the Sun may break through the clouds. The Sun's light then shines through water droplets in the air. That's when you might see a rainbow! Check out those colors: red, orange, yellow, green, blue, indigo, and violet.

TRY IT:

To make a rainbow, you need light and water droplets. Make your own with a garden hose. Stand with your back to the Sun and use the fine spray setting on your hose nozzle. Daisy suggests watering some plants while you do this, so you don't waste the water!

To find a rainbow after a storm, stand with your back to the Sun. Look towards where it is still raining.

Have you seen a rainbow?
Draw what you saw below.

Wait for the thunder to end before you go outside. Try waiting out the storm in a pillow fort!

REFLECTING ON MOONLIGHT

The Moon doesn't make its own light. The Sun's light bounces off of the Moon. When the Moon is full, the sky is bright. You and other living things can see better under the full Moon. When the Moon is new, you don't see the Moon. The night is very dark during a new Moon. It is easier to see the light of more stars. It is a perfect night for stargazing!

Houston, we have a problem. What do you mean there is no cheese on the Moon?

The Moon is made of rock. It is very dry. The Moon has mountains, valleys, and plains, just like Earth. The dark shapes you see on the Moon are craters. Many large and small space rocks made them by crash-landing on the Moon.

Draw the Moon as you see it from home.

TRY IT:

You can make a rocket ship with items around you. You might use a big cardboard box, tape, markers, pots, pans, and pillows. Don't forget to fill up your water bottle and bring snacks. There is no water to drink and no cheese on the Moon. Sorry, Squeeks!

LET'S STOP THE WATER WASTE

All living things need water. It's never a good idea to waste water. It's worse when it hasn't rained in a very long time. Help nature by saving, or conserving, water. Make a poster to remind you of the ways.

Here are a few tips to get you started:

- Shut off the faucet while you brush your teeth.
- Take short showers.
- Check for leaky faucets.

What other ways can you help conserve water?

_____

_____

_____